BIBLE CHICKS

Book 1

By: Khara Campbell

From:
Chandra

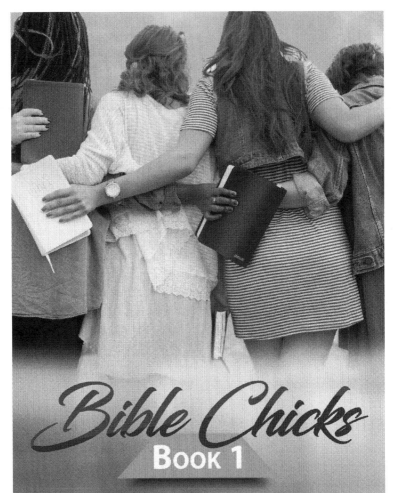

Bible Chicks

BOOK 1

What would women of the bible be like today?

KHARA CAMPBELL

My Thanks

A special thanks to LaKisha Johnson for agreeing to do this project with me. I had envisioned this project one night before bed. I contacted you the next day and without hesitation you were on board. Thank you!!! Working with you on this has been very fulfilling. Thank you to my husband Michael for your excitement about this project, something I needed when I had my moments of doubt.

Synopsis

Have you ever wondered what women in the bible would be like today? How they would act, think, talk and dress? Well, Bible Chicks is a collection of short stories depicting the lives of some courageous biblical women who had the honor of being among few women mentioned in the sacred text.

Their stories are written from today's perspective yet they stay true to the biblical heritage.

It is our hope, by 'updating' their stories, you will get a better understanding of each of the women chosen.

Book one: Woman with the issue of blood, Rehab, Leah and Tamar.

Book two: Gomer, Hannah and Jezebel.

"In the same way, the women are to be worthy of respect, not malicious talkers but temperate and trustworthy in everything."

1 Timothy 3:11 (NIV)

Woman with Issue of Blood

"Veronica"

Matt 9:20-22, Mark 5:25-34, Luke 8:43-48

I stared down at the dark red stain fighting back the tears that were stinging my eyes. Twelve years. Twelve! You would think after so long I would have gotten used to this. Accepted it. But no! Every single day, I was tormented by the constant need of diaper like underwear and dark clothing to hide any accidents I may have. I felt like a prisoner to my condition. For twelve years, I'd been suffering with gynecologic hemorrhage.

My alarm blared again letting me know I needed to get a move on to start my day. I pressed the end button on my cellphone, which sat on the nightstand, stopping the excessively obnoxious sound. Robotically, I peeled the bloody bed pad off my black sheets. Even if a man found interest in me, he probably wouldn't stay with me, having this condition. *Who wanted to be with a woman that bleed every day of her life? Waking up to stained sheets?*

And forget wearing sexy underwear for my husband –
unless Depends came in silk and lace.

I felt like a freak. A circus act. At least that's what it felt like my life had become. Most people wanted nothing to do with me. People that knew of my condition, because I had it since I was thirteen, felt the mere sight of me would get them sick with what they felt was an infectious disease. And because I felt so ashamed of my condition, the ones that wanted to be in my life, I pushed them away.

I only left my house to run quick errands, grocery shopping and to visit my multitude of doctors, that had yet to cure me. Almost all my income, as a closed caption writer, working from my home office, was spent on doctors. My insurance paid little to nothing for my many visits.

I went through my mundane morning routine. Getting rid of the soiled bed pad, changing my black sheets, making sure blood hadn't seeped through the pad and onto my mattress. Then showering, putting on my trusty padded underwear and one of my many black outfits. I decided on black jeans and a plain black t-shirt. I put some product in my naturally curly, shoulder length hair, and combed it through. I looked at myself in the floor length mirror. Perfect. Nothing about me drew unwanted attention to myself—especially with me having to venture out today.

Anxiety kicked in and I closed my eyes to quickly gain control of my wayward thoughts. *You're safe Veronica. You're safe in your home. Breathe. You're going to make your appointment, get some groceries and get back home without any incident. You're stronger than people think. You're not cursed. You're not a freak. Breathe.*

I slowly opened my eyes, looking at my dull reflection. My cellphone started ringing, where I had left it, on my nightstand. For once, I was okay with the distraction of a phone call.

I stared down at my iPhone. My mother was calling. I contemplated letting it go to voicemail, but snatched it up and answered before I talked myself out of it.

"Good morning, Mom," I sat on the edge of my perfectly made bed.

"Veronica? Uh, good morning,"

I caught her off guard by answering the call. I usually sent it to voicemail, listened to her message, then respond by text. I love my mother dearly— but over the years, I've allowed my condition to isolate me from the few people that actually cared about me. My mother certainly wasn't excluded. She meant well and did all she could for me, when I was younger, by taking me to the best doctors and researching the best medication. But I grew tired of what I started to feel was pity, rather than love.

"How are you this morning?"

"I'm okay. I have a doctor's appointment I'm about to head out to."

"Speaking of which, I was calling because I read about this herbal remedy you may want to try."

"Mom…"

"I know, I know. You've tried every remedy under the sun. But this is worth a try, Ronnie. I'll text you the link to the website."

I shook my head as if she could see me but answered, "Okay, I'll check it out."

"Oh good. Let me know how your appointment with Dr. Stevens goes."

As usual, I grumbled under my breath, "Yeah, I will."

"Ok sweetie, I love you!"

"Love you too, Mom. Bye."

Forty-three minutes later, I was walking into my gynecologist office.

"Hey Bloody Ronnie," Beverly, the medical office manager and my friend, said the moment I stepped up to the reception counter. I use the word friend loosely. She and I attended school together, from first grade all the way to twelfth grade. I've told her, and others, numerous times not to refer to me as that. To them, it's a harmless nickname. However, it crushed my soul every time I heard it.

The nickname came about one day in the eighth grade, when I stood up to leave math class and hadn't realized that my light blue pants, had turned crimson red. Unfortunately, I suffered many similar days like that thereafter.

"Hi Bev," My response was sour. I didn't have it in me today to pretend to be sweet.

She raised her, perfectly shaped, brow, that I envied, but allowed my bitterness to slide, "Doctor Harris will be with you shortly." Her response was clipped.

I finished signing in, passing the clipboard to her and walked away from the reception counter to take a seat in the, surprisingly, vacant area. I guess I won't be waiting more than ten minutes to see the doctor today. Where are all the pregnant ladies at? And then my heart clenched. What if I'm never able to have children, because of my condition?

What did I ever do to deserve this curse? Why me?

I quickly sucked up my self-pity. I didn't want to go down that road— at least not there in the doctor's office. Twenty-five years old and I've never been out on a date. Never been kissed and I'll probably die a virgin, because what man would want to put up with my condition? I'll probably die young. I'd been hiding from my mother, the fact that though I'm young, my daily loss of blood was making me weak. Vitamins and other natural remedies helped sustain my health. But I'm tired. So tired. I don't want to keep living like this.

"Veronica Carpenter."

I gather my purse and met the nurse at the door, leading into the examination area. After routinely checking my vitals, I was left in one of the examination rooms waiting for Dr. Stevens.

I used to pray every time I went to the doctors, hoping that one of them would give me the news I desperately wanted to hear—but my prayers has yet to be answered. So, I sat on the exam table, looking aimlessly around at the diagrams and pictures of the female reproductive system.

"The remedy isn't working?"

I shook my head at Dr. Stevens, noticing the care and *pity* in her eyes. "Three months trying the new medication and I'm still soaking my pads, changing them multiple times a day. I still need to sleep with a bed pad at night." I looked away from her, not wanting to see the hopelessness in her eyes. I'm positive mines reflected hers. I'd been to too many doctors to name, she was the only one that kept hope that there was a cure for me.

"How about…"

I held up my hand stopping her, "I'm done. I can't afford to keep putting myself through this. I just need to accept the fact that I'm going to die from this condition. Maybe I need to go on a world trip, I've got years of vacation time stacked up. Leaving Caesarea Philippi for a while, actually seems like a good idea. I've been here all my life, never been on a plane or drove further than two hours away. Maybe in another location people won't look at me like a diseased rat."

"Veronica, a vacation does sound like a great idea. But I don't like the sound of you losing hope. I'm going to continue my research on your condition and contact other specialist worldwide, to help get you a cure, or at the very least some relief."

I slide off the examination table, "Do as you wish, Dr. Stevens. And thank you for trying all these years, I appreciate it. I'll send you a post card," I couldn't bare the look in her eyes, so grabbing my purse, I exited the room.

Leaving in a hurry, I pushed open one of the glass double doors for Doctor Stevens office, and bumped smack dab into someone.

"Watch it, Miss. Are you okay?" The baritone voice was familiar.

I pushed my curls out of my face and looked up into the face of Myron. My high school crush. The man I dreamt of marrying and having four kids with. Two boys and two girls, because it would've been a shame not to replicate more humans like him.

I watched as his expression changed once he realized who I was. "Bloody Ronnie?" He stepped a few inches back in disgust. He looked at the sign on the doctor's office, then back at me. "Bev was right, you still got the plague. You need to watch where you're going, bumping into people trying to spread your curse." He walked passed me with a frown on his face.

Myron quickly reminded me why I was a fool to have had a crush on him and wanted to subject my womb to bearing four of his offspring. *Stupid childhood crush!* I could cuss him out and tell him to rot in hell, but I was emotionally and physically exhausted. Instead, I pressed the key fob to unlock my SUV that was parked right in front of the entrance. I sat in my car, cranking the engine, desperately needing the AC on blast. It was in the high eighties, and the inside of my car was even hotter. My black attire didn't help.

God help me! My desperate prayer slipped. *Who wants to die young? Die like this?* My treacherous eyes followed Myron, dressed in basketballs shorts and a plain t-shirt that he made look very appealing. On his feet, he wore what looked like, expensive tennis shoes. He made dressing down so chic, while I made it look like a science experiment. I watched him approach a woman wearing a sundress.

I couldn't make out her features from the distance, but from what I could see, she was attractive. Super model hot. He pulled her into him, hugging then kissing her. She raised her hand up to fully embrace him, a glint from the sun bounced off, what I could presume, was a diamond ring on her ring finger— I quickly looked away.

I could hear my cellphone ringing in my purse. Again, I was unusually happy for the distraction of a phone call. I dug it out and answered without really looking at who was calling.

"Hello?" I could hear that someone was connected to the call, but they said nothing. "Hello?" I generously offered again.

"Veronica? You answered the phone. I thought mom was kidding when she told me earlier," It was, the second of my two older sisters, Adara.

"It's everyone's lucky day. What's up?" I injected a smile in my voice. I'd become an award-winning actress at hiding my true feelings.

"And you sound cheerful! Does that mean the medication is working? The bleeding stopped?" The excitement in her voice further dampened my mood and made it more difficult to keep up the façade.

I swallowed my emotions, "How's it going, big sis? Did you land that big real estate sale?" She was a commercial realtor.

There was a pregnant pause. And because I enjoyed torturing myself, I looked over toward where I last saw Myron and the pretty woman in the sundress. They must have gone inside of the restaurant that they were standing in front of.

"Actually, that's why I'm calling. Jacomina and I want to celebrate and thought it would be a perfect time for a girls' night. You, me Jacomina and mom. And we're not taking no for an answer, especially with this being our *lucky* day."

I groaned internally, closing my eyes and leaning my head back against the driver's seat headrest. One of the reasons I kept myself isolated, was because I hated the stares and snide comments from people in our large community that really felt small. An incident, when I left a huge red stain on a cloth chair in a restaurant a few years ago, still haunted me. I learned to keep plastic seat covers in my purse because of it. It's like no matter how hard I tried, people only knew me as *Bloody Ronnie*.

"I'm game, if it's a girls' night in," I told her opening my eyes

"Nope. You're going out with us. We have reservations for seven at Peter's, that new seafood restaurant on Bethsaida Drive. We'll pick you up at 6:15, so be ready. Or we'll do it for you."

I groaned again, this time she heard it, "Fine, I'll be ready."

"Oh my goodness! I can't believe it was that easy to convince you. This must be our lucky day. Bye lil sis, love you."

"Love you too, bye."

***

As promised, I was dressed and ready by six wearing an all-black maxi dress with black sandals. No accessories or anything that would make me stand out.

My sister is a stickler for being on time. I watched from the bay window, as Adara pulled into the driveway of my modest home, at exactly 6:15. Her flashy SUV was gleaming in the sun that had yet to set. I picked up my purse from the couch and made my way outside.

"Really, Veronica? Couldn't you have worn anything, other than black?" Jacomina, the older of my two sisters, commented once I got into the car. Mom was riding shotgun. "You're twenty-five years old and walk around like you're in constant mourning."

"This coming from the woman that doesn't need a lifetime supply of depends underwear, or have to carry plastic seat covers in case of accidents! Until you've walked an hour in my shoes, you don't have a say in how I dress."

She looked remorseful, "I get it and I'm sorry. All I was trying to say is, black won't make you invisible, it'll make you stand out." She dug into her purse, "Here, wear these at least."

She placed large gold hoop earrings and a simple, but elegant long gold lariat necklace in my lap.

"And I brought a brush and gel to tame your curls up into a cute ponytail. I just want to see you not looking so down and out all the time, that's all Ronnie."

I looked down at the jewelry, then at my sister, who was already looking at me. She was dressed to kill in a red midi dress and coordinating accessories. Her makeup was flawless and her hair was styled in a chic bob. I could lash out at her, but honestly, although I didn't want to come—I needed to be around my family right now. I turned and saw Adara looking at me through the rearview mirror. Mom's mouth twitched, wanting to say something, but I was happy she decided not to.

"Okay. I'll wear the jewelry and you can style my hair."

"And makeup when we get to the restaurant."

I nodded in agreement.

***

"It's so good to have all my girls together," Mom beamed.

I felt guilty for depriving her of moments like this, because I was always M.I.A.

"Your dad would be proud to see the beautiful ladies you all have grown into."

Our dad died from cancer when I was ten.

"Here's to many more girls' night." She raised her glass of fruity something and we joined in, clinking our glasses together.

For a while, I felt normal. The food was great. Company was awesome and so far, no bloody accidents.

"Mom, Veronica, Jacomina and I invited you both out tonight to share some amazing news," Adara looked across the table to our oldest sister. "You want to go first?"

Jacomina looked like she was about to burst with excitement, "I'm pregnant!"

Mom screamed, drawing attention to our table.

I almost choked on the soda that I was drinking, "Are you serious?" She nodded with an big smile. "Oh my goodness, that's great! I'm going to be an auntie." I pushed my chair back, not doing my habitual check of my seat for stains on the plastic cover first, and bear hugged my sister. "Congratulations Mina!"

"Thank you. David and I are so excited. We wanted to wait until we were in the safe zone before we said anything."

Mom recovered and hugged Jacomina as well. She congratulated her and then began giving her advice on pregnancy.

Adara cleared her throat, "I have some awesome news, too. I closed on the commercial property on Pharaoh Drive yesterday. After the signing, Walden asked me to marry him. I said yes!" She extended her left hand for us to see. She must have slipped the ring on under the table, because we all would've noticed it sooner.

Mom screamed again, but quickly covered her mouth.

With my mouth hanging open, I stared at the exquisite pink diamond ring on Adara's nicely manicured finger. "Congratulations!" I was so happy for her. For both my sisters. "When's the wedding?"

***

The rest of the evening I was in a daze. I couldn't wait to get home. I hugged and kissed my sisters and mom, then made a beeline for my front door. Adara waited for me to enter and turn the lights on, before she reversed out of the yard. After toeing off my sandals, I went into the kitchen and selected a bottle of wine from the wine rack. I chose one that wasn't opened yet. Hastily, I uncorked it and took it to the head. I gulped until the red liquid was spilling down the sides of my mouth, competing with the tears that were running from my eyes.

I sobbed while pulling the bottle from my lips. *Why is everyone's life moving forward and mine is at a stand still? They're living and I'm dying!*

I took the bottle with me out into the living room and plopped down on the couch, where I had it covered with a bed pad. I felt something hard under my bum, then the T.V turned on. I pulled the remote control from under me, tossing it to the side. I gulped some more wine, desperately needing it to work it's magic so I could be numb.

"...he's very controversial, proclaiming to be the only way to God. That he is the way, the truth and life. He's also going up against our traditions—doing things his way. Like healing a man on the Sabbath day. He's also said to have brought a widow's son back to life and turn water into wine. Okay, I need to invite him to my next part," The female newscaster laughed, and her male colleague joined in.

I was literally sitting on the edge of my seat.

"He's also noted for helping fishermen capture a huge number of fish. Talk about a fish fry," The male newscaster commented followed by laughter.

"Minister, Jesus of Nazareth, is noted for performing many miracles and he will be in town tomorrow. That's right folks, you get the chance to hear his teachings yourself and if you're lucky, maybe you can be added to his list of miracles."

Could it be? The wine bottle slipped from my hand, spilling onto the nude carpet. I slid off the couch and crawled to the T.V, staring at the address of where Minister Jesus would be teaching tomorrow. *God, is he the answer to my prayers?* I heard about this man, about his teachings, about his miracles. I *must* be there tomorrow.

People are going to shun you, you can't possibly go. I shook that thought from my head. I've got to go. I stood up. And for the first time in forever —I felt hopeful.

***

I didn't know I had anything other than black in my closet. When I got up that morning I completed my morning routine before walking into my closet to find something to wear. I just couldn't wear black. Not today. I dug through, hoping by some miracle, I had something, at the very least gray, to wear. I was beyond relieved when I found the white sundress, Jacomina bought me two summers ago for an all-white party I refused to attend. It was flowy with spaghetti straps.

I quickly put it on and stood in front of the mirror. It fit me perfectly. I hadn't worn anything, except black, for too many years. I almost didn't recognize myself. Not wanting to allow doubt to overcome me, I raced into the bathroom and applied some of the makeup Jacomina had given me last night to bring life to my dull face. I remembered her quick tutorial in the bathroom of the restaurant and after putting the cap back on the lipstick, I checked myself out in the mirror. *Veronica girl, you look amazing. You've been hiding for far too long.* The most genuine smile brightens my face.

***

My palms were sweaty, and my heart was racing. There were too many people. Too many stares. Too many negative comments. Why did I think dressing in white and applying makeup would make me less noticeable? I leaned over with my hands on my knees, I was having a panic attack. Air, I needed air. Someone shoved me in the back and I almost stumbled. Then, I heard his voice. *Minister Jesus*. His words were the encouragement I needed. I stood back up.

"If I can only touch the hem of his garment," I pushed my way through the crowd. I ignored the stares and sneers. Through the thick of people, I saw him. He stood teaching with his back to me. I pushed further, I stuck my arm out, reaching, reaching until I touched his shirt. I stood still feeling, like a valve being shut off, my hemorrhaging ceased.

"Who touched my clothes?" Jesus asked looking around.

"There are so many people here, it's impossible to know who touched you," His men told him.

Minister Jesus kept asking and I just stood there in shock, awe and gratitude. I went and knelt at his feet, thanking him for what he had done for me. Telling him about my twelve-year condition.

"Your faith has made you whole. Go in peace," He told me with a smile.

I left triumphantly ready for the new chapter in my life.

Rehab

Joshua 2:1-24

Another *very* satisfied customer. I licked my thumb, then proceeded to count the hundred dollar bills that were in my hand and lap. I watched the tall, dark, and beautiful man retreating. He looked over his shoulder giving me a wink before he exited my boudoir. My heart fluttered. I tried to keep feelings out of this business, but sometimes men like him had a crafty way of crossing the barrier I thought I had expertly constructed around my heart. I looked away from him, and back at the stack in my hands.

Twenty G's. Not bad for a night's work. I threw the purple linen sheets back, exposing my size eight naked frame, and climbed out of bed. I stretched and quickly regretted it. My body ached in places I thought were already finely tuned. *I earned every bit of that money*. Nameless worked my body to perfection last night. It's almost a shame I took money from him with all the pleasure he brought me. *Almost a shame.* I'm no dummy. This is my livelihood. If I was using my body to pay my bills and take care of my family, there was no harm in enjoying my profession.

I grabbed the money and placed them in the blue bank deposit bag in my nightstand. I planned on depositing it into the bank right away. First, I needed a shower and then have my housekeeper get to work on changing the sheets and freshen up my boudoir for my next lucky client later this evening.

I was a prostitute, harlot, slut, hoe, just some of the names people used to describe me. But I didn't care. I did what I did to take care of my family. They had a roof over their heads and food to eat every day because of *me*.

I lived in Jericho. A city surrounded by a wall. I owned a six thousand square foot home, that I turned into a bed and breakfast. Perfect cover for my *other* duties. My house sat against the city wall and the roof was level with it. There were stairs on one side of the house that led up to a flat roof that during summer months, I turned into a tropical oasis with above ground pool, jacuzzi and imported tropical plants to set the ambiance. It certainly helped with business. My guests loved it. I had repeat summer clients just because of it.

I also manufactured linen out of flax. And on one part of the roof, was where I stashed my abundance of flax stalks to dry. I had a space in my house dedicated to my passion with all the equipment needed to create and dye fabric. You could say I was a Jane of many trades.

Freshly showered and dressed in my go to yoga pants, cute sleeveless top and jeweled sandals, I was ready to start my day. I had the blue bank bag in hand to quickly deposit it in my bank's night deposit box, although it was currently 4:35 a.m. I needed to make this quick in order to get back in time to prepare breakfast ready for the few guests I had. Especially, the ones checking out before noon.

"Good morning, Rehab," Ella, my housekeeper, said as we approached each other on the stairs. She had an empty hamper in her hand going up as I was coming down. "Early bird catches the worm."

"Can't run my businesses slacking," I said with a smile. She returned it, but it didn't reach her eyes. I knew Ella loved me as if I were her niece. She often called me that, because of our twenty year age difference, and all the loving advice she gives me. However, she didn't like what I did at night. Running a bed and breakfast and manufacturing fabric got her approval, my secret—or not so secret—*profession*, did not. It was frowned upon not only by Ella, but also my biological family, and most of the people in town. I didn't care.

"I noticed your, uh—" she coughed. "*Client* leaving and figured you would be down soon. I'm heading up to change the sheets."

"Thank you. I'm off to the bank I will be back in fifteen minutes to start breakfast."

"Okay. I started coffee already for any early risers. But it seems all of the guests are still in slumber."

***

"...And to other important news this morning. People of Jericho we've reported about the Israelites and their great power and how they claim to be working in the name of God. Conquering our neighboring cities and parting the Red Sea..."

Chop, chop, chop.

I chopped some sweet peppers and other ingredients to add to the omelets I was preparing for breakfast, while listening to the morning news.

"…Since the death of their leader Moses, there is reason to believe his aide, Joshua, has taken his place as leader of the Israelites…"

"What I would like to know is why our King of Jericho hasn't prepared the military for a potential war?" A second commentator said. "The Israelites believe that Jericho is part of the land their God will give to them. And if we don't prepare to fight, we're doomed."

With a knife suspended in air, my attention was fully on the T.V. screen, that was mounted on wall ahead of me, right above the breakfast nook.

From the men, that pass-through and stayed at my bed and breakfast, I'd heard many things about the Israelites, Moses and the God they serve, and I'd been very fascinated. How powerful is such a God to part a sea?

"Good morning," came the soft voice of a woman in her early sixties, followed by her equally aged husband, walking into the kitchen. "It smells delightful in here."

Smiling, I placed the knife down on the cutting board, "A great morning to you, Mr. and Mrs. Jacobs. Did you sleep well last night?"

Mr. Jacobs nodded at me with a pleasant smile.

Mrs. Jacobs answered, "Oh but of course, dear. Your accommodations have been lovely these past two days. I hate it that we have to leave this morning."

With the town's people shunning me because of my secret profession, it didn't hurt my bed and breakfast business because my clientele were all out-of-towners. Same for my fabric manufacturing business, most of my sales were from online buyers that I shipped to globally.

I picked up the TV remote and muted the voice of the newscasters, though I really wanted to hear more about Joshua and the Israelites and the potential war. I would just do some more research on my own later.

"Are you in the mood for omelets for breakfast? I also have fresh fruits, waffle mix ready for the waffle machine and sausage and bacon in the warmers. And of course, there's a variety of cereals to choose from."

"I'll take an omelet please, with all that good stuff you have chopped up," Mr. Jacobs answered making his way toward the waffle machine.

***

The front door chimed notifying me that someone had entered the foyer. Pulling my attention away from my laptop screen, where I was replying to a fashion designer regarding a special order of linen fabric. The pile of flax I had drying on the roof were just what I needed to create her order. I pushed away from my desk and stood to walk to the reception counter. I had it specially made and placed in the foyer of my home to assist guests with checking in and out. From the looks of the two men that entered, I was guessing they were looking to rent some rooms, though they weren't carrying any luggage. Luckily, I had two rooms available.

Both men, dressed casually in all black, were quite attractive too. Perhaps I would have the pleasure of warming both their beds tonight.

"Good evening, gentlemen," I greeted them sweetly, discreetly pushing my c-cup breasts up to make them even more desirable in my V-neck top. "Looking for a place to stay?"

To my disappointment my little act didn't seem to sway them. By now, I had most men drooling from my presence alone. These two weren't even looking directly at me, they were scoping out my place as if I had roaches. Which I certainly didn't. I ran a five-star bed and breakfast.

Hmmm, interesting.

"Yes ma'am. We need two rooms please," The taller of two men answered with an accent I hadn't heard before. I'd heard many, but his was different.

"Sure. You're in luck. I have two available. I'll just need your credit card and ID..."

"Good, we'll take them. But we'll pay in cash. And unfortunately, we don't have any identification on us at the time," The slightly shorter man replied with the same accent.

Something about these men are different.

"No worries. Cash is the *perfect* form of payment. Can I have your names at least?"

The taller of the two shook his head, "Just call us John and Doe, ma'am. I'll be John."

Any other time, I probably should've been alarmed by the evasiveness of the men renting a room in my home, but something about their odd presence was calming.

"Okay, *John*. The fee is $125 a night."

He pulled his wallet from the back pocket of his jeans and thumbed a few bills, before handing them over to me. Three hundred dollars. "We only need rooms for one night. Keep the change."

"Thank you!" I quickly placed the cash in the register. "Come, let me show you your rooms. Do you want to get your luggage from your vehicle first?"

Doe shook his head, "Please, just show us where we'll be spending the night."

***

"Have you heard?" Ella asked, as I assisted her with loading the dishwasher. The three guests, who had came down for dinner, were long gone.

"Heard what?" After placing the last dish in, I shut the door to the machine and started it.

She began to whisper, looking over her shoulder as if someone else was in the kitchen with us, "People are saying the King believes some

Israelite spies have come to spy out the land to take charge of it."

Could it be?

My heart sunk down to my toes. I gripped the countertop to keep my balance. I hadn't told Ella about the two men who had rented rooms that evening. They begged me to keep their presence under wraps, and as one always wanting to please my clients, I agreed. I had taken dinner up to them earlier, without Ella noticing. As far as she knew, those room were off limits. And with my secret profession, she understood why that rule was in place.

"Rehab, are you okay?" Ella came quickly to my aid, walking me over to sit on a stool. "You look faint."

"I'm...I'm okay. I must be a little faint from all the hours I spent on my feet today dying that scarlet fabric. It's was difficult getting the perfect shade of red."

Ella goes to fetch me some water from the dispenser on the fridge, "If I haven't told you once, I've told you a trillion times, to take a break and eat when you're up in your lab." She returned with a full glass of water and passed it to me.

"Thank you," I took a sip, hoping it would calm my nerves. *Israelite spies? Are they truly men of God? Men who worship the same God of Moses and Joshua? What blessing do I have, a sinner like me, to house two men of God? I must warn them!* "I know, you're right. I will do better next time."

"Oh, you will all right. I will come up there myself and force feed you if I have to," She watched me take a few more sips until she was satisfied. "You go on to bed. I will finish up what's left and turn in myself."

I nodded, not trusting myself to speak. Leaving the glass on the counter, I hurriedly walked out of the kitchen.

Knock, knock, knock.

"Mr. John!"

I stepped over to the other door nearby.

Knock, knock, knock.

"Mr. Doe!" I whisper-screamed hoping to get their attention, but not to alarm the other guests. My heart was galloping in my chest. I rubbed my sweaty palms against the seams of my yoga pants.

"Rehab, what is it?" John was now standing in the doorway. The sound of Doe opening his bedroom door followed. They were both still fully dressed in all black.

"The King of Jericho knows that you're in town. You must hide, quickly!"

Doe looked at me peculiarly, "How do you know who we are?"

"I knew there was something different about you two earlier. Now everything is adding up. Are you truly men of God?"

They both nodded.

"Then come! You must hide up on my roof, " I started down the hallway towards the secret entrance to the roof, from the second floor, that was off limits to guests. John and Doe followed behind me.

When we reached the roof, John looked at me with uncertainty, "Are you sure we will be safe up here?"

"I hope so. You can hide under these stalks of flax. It's perfect!"

I wrung my hands with worry making sure the men were completely covered under the flax before I left the roof.

I couldn't sleep with torment. I was boring a hole in my hardwood floors. At 10:15 p.m, the doorbell rang. I was already on the main floor with the TV on having anxiety over what was going to happen next. I quickly answered the door, knowing it was the police.

"Ma'am," the officer greeted, well actually a CIA agent according to his badge. There were about ten police officers behind him. Their police cars overwhelmed my large paved driveway. Thankfully, they weren't flashing red and blue lights. The last thing I needed, was them drawing unwanted attention my way. "We have reason to believe two men, whom we believe are spies, have rented rooms in your home. We need to take them into custody, now."

"Oh…uh…well, two men did come here earlier and rented rooms, but for whatever reason, they checked out and left a little after eight tonight. They were very evasive, they wouldn't even tell me their names and they paid in cash. I'm not sure exactly where they are headed, but I think I heard one of them mentioning heading west."

"They must have figured out that we had intel on them being in town. Good, we'll head west and sniff them out."

I stood in the doorway frozen, until I could no longer see the taillights of the police cars. I closed and locked the front door taking a shuddering breath. *I could go to jail, or worse, be killed for treason.* I leaned my back against the door with my eyes closed and steadied my breathing.

Fully composed, I dashed up to the roof where the two spies were still hiding under the stalks of flax.

"John...Doe. They're gone." I whispered just enough for them to hear me. I watched as both men peaked their heads out from under the flax stalks. "I know that the Lord has given you Jericho, and because of it, everyone is afraid of war. We've all heard of the miraculous things your God has done. Parting the red sea for you when you left Egypt, your victory over the two kings of the Amorites east of the Jordan. Everyone here was so fearful when we heard about it, because your God is very powerful. Your God is the God of heaven above and the earth below. So, I need you to promise me, that you will spare me and my family when you conquer the land. You will show kindness to me, because I've shown kindness to you. Please let me know that you will spare me and my entire family? That we won't die in the war."

Doe walked over to me, his all black outfit fully covered in lint from the flax, "Our lives for your lives."

"Promise," John confirmed, dusting the lint off himself. "Keep all of this a secret, and you and your family will be safe."

I wiped away the tears from my cheeks, just then realizing I was crying, "Thank you!"

"We've got to get out of here," Doe walked over to the edge of the roof that was against the city wall looking for a way down.

When I first moved in this house, I thought it was kind of odd to have my roof level with the city wall, then I thought it added character, now I saw its true purpose. To help these men of God.

"Come, you can get down through this window that's through the city wall using this cloth. I will quickly rope it together." I picked up the cloth, I had dyed that day then brought up to the roof to air dry near the pool. I took it to the window. "I'm sure this is more than enough for you to reach the ground on the other side. Go towards the hills so the police won't find you. Hideout for about three days until they return, then go back where you came from."

Both men looked at me thoughtfully, "Before we leave, we need you to understand, for us to keep our promise to you, we need a signal from you when we return." John eyed the scarlet fabric. "Hang scarlet curtains in your windows. Bring all your family to live with you and during the war, they must not leave the house. If anyone leaves, we won't be responsible if their lives are lost. But if anyone inside your home is injured we will be held responsible. If you tell your government about us, the deal is off!"

"I will do what you say and keep your promise. I won't tell anyone."

"Good," John smiled and for the first time, I felt he actually looked at me. I mean *really* looked at me, like I was a woman worthy of being a Queen. No man had ever looked at me like that. "Before we leave, I must properly introduce myself. My name is Salmon." He extended his hand to me, his strong muscular hand. I looked at it then into his beautiful chocolate eyes. And for what seemed like the first time, I was speechless around a man.

I heard Doe chuckle, but my eyes were still glued to who I now knew as Salmon. "My name is Gavi, and Salmon and I need to go now."

"Oh, yes of course. It was nice to officially be introduced to you both," I finally shook Salmon's hand that was still proffered to me. He smiled, and my heart melted. "Please be safe."

"We will. And you."

Salmon and Gavi climbed down the rope, then I quickly brought it back up through the window. I watched them run off into the night, one taking my heart with him.

God of Moses and Joshua, please guide and protect them and keep your people and my family safe. Forgive me of my sins, Lord. Cleanse my heart. I want to be your servant.

As promised, my family and I were spared in the war. And sometime later, Salmon and I married and bore a son named Boaz. Boaz married Ruth, their son was Obed. Jesse was the son of Obed and the father of David, through which lineage, Jesus was born.

I was once a harlot but through faith, I became part of the genealogy of Christ the Lord.

Leah

Genesis 29; 30; 49:31

I loved my little sister Rachel dearly, she was my first best friend. We were inseparable as youngsters. As her big sister, she wanted to do everything I did and go everywhere I went, and I didn't mind. But I also envied her. Sometimes, it pained me to look at her. She and I could've passed for twins, but I was cursed with a lazy eye. As we matured, her beauty became more defined and my faults we're terrifyingly highlighted. I was the ugly duckling, which was made significantly evident by the fact that no one wanted to marry me.

"Jacob has worked for me seven years, because I promised he could marry my youngest daughter, Rachel. But Leah is the oldest and by custom, she must be married first," Laban, my father said after blowing smoke into the air.

"What are you saying, Laban? You're going to make him marry the ugly one?" My uncle asked, as they chatted on the back porch while smoking cigars.

They must have thought the house was empty, because I had told dad I was going shopping at the mall and Rachel had went to a party with some friends. My uncle's description of me wasn't new, but it still hurt to hear it. I leaned against the closed French door listening in. Their backs were to me, where they sat facing the large pool.

"I have no choice. It's custom for the first daughter to wed, you know this."

"I do, but you will be going back on your word. And how will you pull this off? You know Jacob wants nothing to do with Leah. She's my niece, but it's even hard for me to look her in the face."

"I have a plan, hopefully it works."

I stood their giddy with excitement. I will get to marry Jacob. Oh, how I love that man. From the moment daddy invited him to live with us on the estate, I had dreamed of being his wife and the mother of his children. But it was like I was invisible to him. All he saw was Rachel. Rachel, Rachel, Rachel! She had so many men after her that Jacob was just another admirer added to her long list. She cared nothing for him, but he wanted her and not me.

If daddy's plan, whatever it was, worked—I would be married to the man of my dreams. I walked away from the French doors with a skip in my step.

Two days before the planned wedding for my sister and Jacob, I had given up hope. I sat in the middle of my bed with puffy red eyes. I was all cried out. Daddy had yet to come to me about his plan to trick Jacob into marrying me, and I didn't have the guts to tell him that I overheard him and uncle talking. I needed for him to tell me his plan.

I wiped the snot from my nose. Maybe daddy changed his mind. Uncle was right, daddy couldn't go back on his word to Jacob.

There was a rapid knock on my bedroom door. I quickly gathered the snotty and wet tissues off the comforter and shoved them underneath. I sniffled and wiped underneath my eyes with my fingers.

"Yes!" I called out to the knocker.

I watched the doorknob turn and in walked my dad, so tall and strong in stature. Rachel inherited her good looks from both our parents, I had no clue where my lazy eye and ugliness came from. Talk about skipping generations.

"Leah, sweetheart..." Daddy stopped when he saw me on the bed, I must have looked a wreck. "Are you all right?"

I nodded my head, still not brave enough to confront him about his plan anymore.

"Okay," He went and sat on the arm chair adjacent to my queen bed. "As you know, you are the oldest daughter, and it is custom for the oldest daughter to marry first."

I nodded.

"I'm not allowing Jacob to marry Rachel, not until you're married."

"But...there's no man interested in taking me out on a date, let alone proposing to marry me."

Daddy nodded, "That is why I need you to dress in Rachel's wedding gown and keep your veil on the entire time."

I faked being shocked, "What? Are you serious? How could he not know I'm not Rachel?"

"We will just tell him it's our custom for the bride to keep on her veil until after…" Daddy coughed. "Until after you…ya know."

I nodded, not trying to hide my smile. *I know!*

"Good. So, will you do it?"

"Yes, Daddy! I will do it."

"Good, good," He stood. "I will have the maid assist you with everything on the wedding day."

***

Rachel's wedding gown was gorgeous. She did a great job picking out the white lace masterpiece. Good thing she and I wore the same size. I almost felt guilty for making it my own, but I knew I loved Jacob more than Rachel ever would. Actually, I don't think she had any strong feelings for him, so I was doing them both a favor. Somehow, Daddy convinced Rachel that the wedding was put off for a couple weeks and sent her on a quick getaway with friends.

Through my veil, I saw Jacob looking debonair waiting for me at the altar. He had a megawatt smile brightening his handsome face. I couldn't believe I was living out my fantasy. Jacob looked at me like I was the most precious thing he'd ever seen. No one had ever looked at me like that. And even though the look wasn't truly for me, I was taking it as my own.

After professing our love and commitment to each other, Jacob lifted my veil slightly, only to reveal my red covered lips, and sealed our matrimony with a kiss.

"I can't wait to truly make you all mine tonight," Jacob whispered in my ear, sending a tremble down my spine.

I was anxious for our wedding night for so many reasons. I was tempted many times to take off the veil to get a better view of the Adonis that laid seductively on the king-sized bed. This was so much better than I imagined. So. Much. Better!

I was dressed in a nude negligee that showcased all my assets. I may not have had a pretty face, but the rest of me looked and functioned perfectly. At least I hope it did. The lustful look in Jacob's eyes quickly erased my doubt.

"You are so beautiful, Rachel. I've waited seven years to make you my wife and it was worth every second."

I met him at the foot of the bed. His hands traced my body, then his mouth followed.

***

"Whoa!" was followed by a loud thud, when Jacob fell out of the bed after seeing me without my veil on. He stood up looking down at me with contempt. "What...what are you doing here? Where is my wife, Rachel?"

I sat up in the bed not bothering to cover my nakedness. He'd seen and had the pleasure of it all last night, "Rachel was never here, I'm your wife."

"What? NO! Laban promised me Rachel. Not..." He couldn't look at me any further, giving me his back. "Not you." He went into the bathroom slamming the door behind him.

I flinched from the impact. Tears prickled my eyelids. *How did I think I could make him love or want me?*

I followed Jacob home to confront my father.

"You deceived me, Laban! Leah was not part of the deal?" Jacob barged into dad's home office.

Daddy said a few words to the person on the phone then hung it up, "Jacob, please sit."

"No! I want to know why you deceived me? I don't want Leah as my wife, I worked seven years for you for Rachel."

"Yes, I know, but it's not custom for the youngest daughter to marry before the older. If you promise to work for me another seven years, I will give you Rachel as your wife also."

I stood in the doorway completely conflicted. I will remain Jacob's wife, but I would have to share him with Rachel. I guess we're the definition of the term sister-wives. I hated the idea, but at least he was still mine.

***

I was an emotional nutcase the day of Jacob's marriage to my sister. I refused to be present. If she had come to me about being a bridesmaid, I would've lost it on her. I was beyond irritable and a bitch to everyone, but I couldn't help it. Jacob was *my* husband and Rachel deserved no part of him!

I heard their marriage went off without a hitch. To punish myself further, I snuck and watched them at the reception. Jacob was so enamored with Rachel. The way he looked at her, touched her, and the way she put a genuine smile on his face, made me feel even less than I've ever felt in my life.

Why couldn't he love *me*?

If having Rachel as his wife made him happy, I had no choice but to accept their union. His happiness meant everything to me.

***

Rachel sat on the couch with her feet curled up underneath her. She was fully engrossed in the reality TV show on the wide flat screen, that hung above the fireplace.

I plugged in the vacuum cleaner, "Aren't you going to help clean, so our husband doesn't come home to a dirty house?"

She shook her head and added, "No."

"What about cooking? Jacob needs to come home to a homecooked meal after working hard all day."

"You know I don't like cooking. Besides, I texted him a moment ago to bring me takeout for dinner."

I grinded my teeth.

She laughed at something on the television and I turned on the vacuum cleaner, with her giving me the stink eye. *Good! Get your lazy butt up and do something more productive.*

She just sat there and turned up the volume. I wished I could suck her into the vacuum cleaner like the filth she was.

After cleaning the house, doing the laundry and making sure Jacob had clean clothes, I took my time making him a homecooked meal of steak, potatoes and a Caesar salad. Promptly that evening, I heard Jacob pulling into the driveway. I took off my apron and went to the door, that led to the garage to greet him.

"Welcome home, honey!" I said with a smile.

He grumbled a hello and sidestepped me, when I went to hug him. He placed a greasy brown paper bag on the counter then left the kitchen. I followed him to the living room, where Rachel was still sitting on the couch watching TV.

"Hey sweetheart, I brought you dinner liked you asked, why did you cook dinner? Whatever it is smells great." Jacob flopped down next to Rachel, pulling her into his lap. She threw her arms around him before, he passionately kissed her.

I stood there speechless like the third wheel I was.

"Yeah, dinner does smell good. Leah said she was cooking something. We can eat that instead. I'll leave the takeout for lunch tomorrow."

"Sounds good to me, as long as I can have you as dessert later," He bit her passionately on the neck.

I left them and went back into the kitchen to get Jacob's plate ready for dinner.

Jacob made love to Rachel multiple times before putting her to sleep. I needed to move into one of the other bedrooms that weren't close to hers. I couldn't take the torture much longer, it was a miracle I lasted this long. I wiped the tears from my eyes before resting my head against the pillow. A few moments passed, before I heard the knob to my room door turning. I sat up anxiously watching Jacob enter. His hair looked wet from a shower. He was bareback and only wearing boxer shorts. He wordlessly slipped into bed with me. I allowed him to have his way with my body, keeping my eyes closed so he wouldn't have to look at my lazy eye. It was a few short minutes before he was filling me with his seed and then rolling off me and drifting to sleep.

The day I found out I was pregnant, was on the short list of happiest days of my life. Especially, because me being Jacob's first wife *I* would be blessing him with his first child. This was something Rachel couldn't take from me.

Thank you, God, for this blessing! Maybe now Jacob will love me.

"I'm pregnant!" I exclaimed excitedly.

Jacob looked at me blankly, from where he sat across from me at the dining table. Rachel was sitting beside him to his right.

"Oh...okay."

With just two letters he deflated the happiness bubbled up inside me.

He turned expectantly at Rachel, "What about you, babe, are you pregnant?"

Rachel shook her head replying, "No." I couldn't muster any ounce of compassion for the sadness in her voice.

Jacob placed a comforting hand atop Rachel's, "Don't worry sweetheart, God will bless us with a child."

I pushed away from the table and stormed off.

Tamar

Genesis 38

I hummed along to the choir singing. I was too choked up to do more than that. I lifted my veil, attached to my hat and dabbed the corners of my eyes. On either side of me, in the pew, sat my father in law, Judah, and my brother in law, Onan. My younger brother in law, who was in his early teens, sat beside Judah and his mother, Shuah. My husband's dead body laid in the casket before us and looked nothing like the man I knew.

I hated funerals, especially when I had to see the dead body. Er died of a heart attack a few days ago. As far as I knew, he was the picture of perfect health, then I got the call that he was found dead, hunched over his office desk. I wondered if someone had him poisoned and it induced the heart attack. I loved Er dearly, but he was a wicked man. He'd ruined many people's livelihood, because of his hostile takeover of struggling businesses and tearing down low-income housing districts, to put up high-rise buildings with quadrupled the rent. He was a shark and didn't care who he bit. But he was still my husband and I mourned his death. I wished we had more time together, so I could've bore him a child, now he was gone without an heir.

Not many people showed up to Er's funeral. They were probably having celebrations because of his death. I even received a few congratulation cards in the mail. After the funeral service and burial, there was a small gathering at the house in his honor. That, I enjoyed. Reminiscing about his life and the brief time I had with my beloved.

Judah was a very traditional man. Er was the first of his three sons and he wanted his oldest to have a heir. I felt the same way, and as the widow to his son, it was Judah's responsibility to take care of me.

A couple days after the funeral, I overheard Judah and Onan talking in the study, in the home I shared with them.

"With your brother dead, it will be your duty to marry Tamar and have a child that will carry on your brother's name," Judah sat comfortably in one of the chairs facing the couch that Onan sat on.

Judah was a beautiful man. Strong and studious. He looked much younger than he actually was. Onan, like Er, resembled their father.

I inched closer to the cracked door to get a better view and listened clearly without being seen or heard.

Onan shook his head, "Do you hear what you're asking me? To marry and sleep with my brother's wife. And to have a child that won't be considered my own?"

"It's part of your duty as the second oldest. It's our law, you must do it! Er's name must be carried on. Besides, Tamar is gorgeous, courageous and smart, she will be a wonderful wife to you, as she was to your brother."

"And what about my name? I'm supposed to get Tamar pregnant and raise a child I can't call my own?"

Judah stood abruptly, "It is tradition and you will not fail me!" He started for the door and I quickly walked away, hiding around the corner, not to be seen.

***

I stood, for the second time, in front of a minister wearing a white dress. I was happy with the fact that Judah was fulfilling his obligation to me and having Onan marry me. I had to have a child to carry on Er's name and it would be through his brother.

Onan had a sour face the entire ceremony. He didn't even turn to look at me, as I walked down the aisle toward him. I understood, to some degree, his grievance—but we were fulfilling tradition. This was our duty.

"Onan, do you take, Tamar, to be your lawfully wedded wife?" The minister asked. The entire church was silent as if they all sensed Onan's hesitance.

I stared up at him, he looked down at me with a frown on his face. He went to say something, but bit down on his lip to prevent whatever it was from slipping between them. He turned his head and looked at his father, Judah, sitting proudly in the first pew. Judah nodded, an encouragement or warning to Onan. Onan turned back to look at me and finally spoke.

"I do," He said it so softly, even the minister had to ask for him to repeat it. "I do!"

I felt like I could finally breathe. I promised that day to be the perfect wife to my new husband. I would love, honor and respect him. The promised was sealed with a kiss.

***

Hearing that Onan had entered the honeymoon suite, I busied myself in the bathroom rubbing enticing oil over my body. A store clerk had vowed by it, when my girlfriends and I were in the lingerie store earlier that week. I went to the spa the day before and had my body waxed. I slipped on the white negligee and red pumps. I checked myself out in the full length mirror and was very impressed. My skin glowed. My size eight frame should be very appeasing for my husband tonight. I pulled the pins out of my thick kinky tresses, letting it fall over my shoulders. I finger combed it some. I turned every which way in the mirror, self-approving every angle.

Hopefully we make a baby tonight.

I stepped out the bathroom, standing in the door frame, I had captured Onan's full attention. He was sitting on the edge of the bed still wearing his tux, minus the jacket. No trace of disgust or despair was in his eyes, only pure lust. I stepped over to my cellphone I had left on the dresser. Onan followed me with his eyes. I pressed a few buttons, then the sound of slow jams began to play.

I turned, finding Onan right before me. He stared down at me, biting on his bottom lip—that within seconds, were all over me. We made love thoroughly, but as soon as we were done he was off me, covering himself. I saw drops of his semen on his hand right before it slipped to the floor. I hoped that I captured some of it within me.

Some time passed but our lovemaking remained the same. Every single time, Onan cheated me of the chance of conceiving a child. I was heartbroken, but what could I do? He didn't want to fulfill his obligation—a child to the tribe of Judah.

I was beginning to think I may be cursed. Or maybe God wasn't approving of the men I married.

"Tamar...Onan, he's dead! Tamar your husband is dead!"

I sank to the floor clutching the phone to my ear, "What? How?" I sobbed.

"It looks like it may have been a heart attack. Someone found him slumped over in the elevator," Onan's secretary told me. He had taken over Er's business and continued with the same heartless practices.

I wiped the snot from my nose with my hand that was covered in flour. I was in the kitchen kneading bread when she called. I dreaded having to tell Judah and Shuah their second son was dead, if they hadn't heard the news already.

***

Judah was dealing with a lot of grief, which I understood when he told me to go back and live with my father. He promised when his youngest, Shelah, was old enough to marry I would return. Though I had a feeling I shouldn't hold my breath on that promise. What if he felt I was cursed too, that what happened to Er and Onan because of their marriage to me, the same fate would fall on his only living son?

I left Judah's home and returned to live with my father. Years passed and no word from Judah. I knew

Shelah was old enough now for me to marry, but it seemed Judah broke his promise with me. I dutifully waited like he promised and maybe I should've just left it alone, but something within me knew I had to bare a child in the tribe of Judah. I just had too!

Judah's wife died, and I sent my condolences, since I didn't find out until after she was buried. He's had a tough few years and maybe me showing up wasn't a good thing.

After a long day on my feet working in my father's pharmacy as a pharmacy tech, I deserved to lay back and relax. After a hot shower, I got comfortable on my bed and started flipping channels to find something interesting to watch.

I settled on a romantic comedy, then my cellphone ding with an incoming text message. It was a text from my best friend.

Kaija: Girlllll, I heard your father in law heading up to Timnah. Did you know he was in town?

Me: No, I didn't know. Are you sure?

Kaija: Yeah, that's what I heard from Wade. He said Judah was going to look at his farm. You know Wade shears his sheep.

Me: Okay. Thanks for the heads up.

Kaija: Just thought you should know. I knew you were concerned about him since his wife passed.

Me: Yeah. Thanks again ☺

Judah was in town. Maybe, maybe this is the opportunity I needed. He hasn't kept his promise and I deserve a reason why.

Hopping out of bed, I dashed to my closet looking for the perfect outfit. I pulled on a sexy black party dress with nude heeled sandals. In the bathroom, I applied dramatic makeup with contours that gave me a different, but still beautiful appearance. All I needed next was a wig, one the complete opposite of my natural hair. Thankfully, I found a red hair wig, Kaija, left here some time ago when she used me as a dummy for her custom wigs business.

I couldn't get two steps without a man whistling at me.

"Baby, baby, baby, let me be your man tonight!"

"Hmmhmm, sweet thang. That dress sure looks good on you."

"Is your hair red everywhere baby? I sure would like to find out."

"Honey, I would drink your bath water, as long as I can have you as dessert later."

One was bold enough to tug on my arm, "Sweet thaaang, let me make all your dreams come true."

My nosed turned up smelling the stench of alcohol on his breath, "No thank you, I'll be taking care of that myself." I yanked my arm away from his sweaty grip.

"Y-your loss," I watched him stumbling away.

I stood on the corner, watching every vehicle that went by, searching for that one black one with a distinctive license plate. Sun was still up at this time of the evening, which made it easier to read the plates.

I was about to give up, my feet were burning in the sandal heels, and although the sun was starting to set, the heat was becoming unbearable. I searched in my purse for my cellphone to text Kaija, I needed confirmation if what she heard about Judah passing through was correct.

A horn blowing, startled me and I almost dropped my phone on the sidewalk. I looked up to find that a sleek, black sedan, had pulled up to the curb. The window rolled down and Judah's face became visible. My heart started pounding in my chest. *Does he recognize me?*

"How much for your services tonight, beautiful?"

I stared at him openmouthed, I came up with this hairbrained plan on a whim—but to see it working, threw me for a loop.

"We can discuss payment later. It will be worth your while," I finally replied, with what I hoped was a seductive smile.

Judah smirked the winked, "Something tells me you will be work every penny. Get in."

I was a nervous wreck sitting in the car next to him. He tried to make small talk on the way to his hotel, but I couldn't. I simply nodded or shook my head at certain questions. I was also worried he may recognize my voice, so I tried a slightly different accent.

Walking into his hotel room, my nerves were starting to get the best of me, but I had to go through with this—*this may be my only shot.*

"What will you give me to sleep with you?"

"I'll send you a car from my fleet," I could tell he was undressing me with his eyes from where we stood in the middle of the room, near the king size bed.

"I need you to give me something as a promise, that you will send the car."

"What do you need as proof that I will keep my word?"

I knew exactly what I wanted, but I looked him over to go along with the act. "Your ring with those initials on it and…your cane."

Judah slid the ring off his finger. "Fine. It's yours and the cane, until I deliver your car."

I accepted both, placing the ring safely in my purse and putting his cane near my purse on the dresser. With my back to him, I took a deep breath, turned to face him then seductively strutted over to him.

"Let me give you a night you will never forget."

3:15 a.m the next morning, I slid from the bed where Judah slept peacefully. I stared down at my father-in-law, hoping that he would forgive me for deceiving him, and that by some miracle he got me pregnant.

***

"What have you done?" My father's voice boomed from behind. I had just stepped out of my bathroom from vomiting my guts out.

I nervously turned to face him, standing in the doorway to my bedroom. "Wh-what are you talking about?"

"Your mother is convinced you're pregnant, she's seen you throwing up a lot recently and you've gained some weight."

I thought I was doing a good job at hiding it. I wasn't ready to let anyone know yet.

"Are you pregnant?"

I nodded.

"So, you're the prostitute people were talking about, that was walking the streets three months ago?"

I nodded.

My father angrily ran a hand over his face, then stormed away leaving me standing there bewildered and afraid of what was to come.

"Here she is, Judah, your daughter-in-law that got pregnant by being a prostitute. She's brought shame to your family."

I stood before Judah in his study, literally shaking in my shoes. I felt like I was in a scene of one of those mafia movies. Judah sat astute in the high back chair, behind a large mahogany desk, with a few of his men standing beside him.

"What you have done warrants death, Tamar. Not only have you brought shame to my household but your father's as well. What do you have to say for yourself?"

I nervously walked toward his desk and placed his ring and cane atop it, "These belong to the father of my baby."

Judah looked down at the items, his hand reaching for the gold ring, he looked at me with sorrow and regret, "I failed you. I acted out of lust when I slept with you, but you did what you did because of my betrayal. Your life will be spared, and no harm will come to you or your child."

"Thank you!" I smiled gratefully.

Months later I gave birth to twin boys: Perez and Zerah. I didn't know it at the time, and my actions could be seen as scandalous, but through our son

Perez, Judah and I became ancestors to Christ Jesus.

Book Club/Bible Study Questions

1. Which Bible chick did you relate to more and how?

2. Which Bible chick did you relate to the least?

3. Which Bible chick was most inspiring and why?

4. Which story was the most scandalous?

5. What are some similarities you see with Veronica, Rehab, Leah and Tamar?

6. Why do you think Tamar was so determined to get pregnant and carry on the lineage of the tribe of Judah?

7. Do you think Judah's last son would've died too had he married Tamar?

8. Even though Leah went along with tricking Jacob into marrying her, do you think he was justified in the way he treated her?

9. Why were these women significant in the bible?

10. How has God spoke to you through these women's story?

THANK YOU FOR READING!!!!

I hope you enjoyed reading Bible Chicks as much as I did writing it.

Please do me a HUGE favor and leave a review where you purchased.

All the best to you!!!!!

Made in the USA
Lexington, KY
18 December 2019